흐르고 흔들리는 기쁨

Flowing and Shaking Joy

이 향 영 畵詩集 (Lisa Lee)

흐르고 흔들리는 기쁨

초판1쇄 발행 | 2024년 6월 20일

지 은 이 | 이향영
번   역 | 이승희
펴 낸 이 | 배재경
편 집 디 자 인 | 조민지
펴 낸 곳 | 도서출판 작가마을
등   록 | 제 2002-000012호
주   소 | (48931) 부산광역시 중구 대청로141번길 3 (중앙동. 501호 다온빌딩)
           서울시 도봉구 도당로 82(방학1동. 방학사진관 3층)

ISBN 979-11-5606-258-5 3810   정가 20,000원

흐르고 흔들리는 기쁨

Flowing and Shaking Joy

이향영 지음

Lisa Lee

도서출판
작가마을

축복과 기쁨으로 보내니,
꽃처럼 고운 미소가 날아든다

《흐르고 흔들리는 기쁨》 이란 화집畫詩集,
마지막이 될 가슴으로, 그분 안에서
노을의 그림자를 영혼으로 보듬는다.

정리의 계절이 발등까지 와 있는데
머뭇거릴 시간은 욕망을 붙잡는 듯, 두 눈에 어리는 눈물...
그대라면 단호히 뿌리칠 수 있겠는가?

이미 사전연명의료의향서에 등록하여
인제대학교 의과대학에 기증될
나의 주검에 대한 등록증이 나와 있다.

떠나는 길목에 걸림돌 하나 없겠나 했는데
마지막으로 정리하지 못한,
가슴과 생각이 별처럼 박혀있는 그림들이 남아 있었다.

미국에서 개인전을 했고

언젠가는 또 하리라 간직했던 그림들,
그러나 이제는 떠나보내기 위해, 조카 선문과 촬영을 했다.

마음이 흐르고, 흔들려서 그림이 비뚤어졌으나
부끄러운 속내 들켜도 어쩌지 못하는 그리움

《흐르고 흔들리는 기쁨》 그림 시집에 추억을 담았고,

새 주인을 만나게 될, 나의 분신 같은 그림들
이제는 축복과 기쁨으로, 보내고자 마음을 다독이니
비로소 꽃처럼 고운 미소가 찾아든다.

이제는 아쉬움을 훌훌 털고 흘려보낼 수 있으리라!

2024년 5월 해운대에서

저자 이향영 Lisa Lee

When freeing with blessings and joy,
         a gracious flowery smile flies in

The painting poem collection Flowing and Shaking Joy,
Thinking in my heart will be the last, in Him
The shadow of the sunset I embraced with my soul

The season to wrap up is just around the corner yet
It seems time to hesitate holds on to desire, tears welling
in both eyes...
If it were you, could you firmly shake it off?

Already signed the Advance Letter for the Matter of Pro
longing Life
Already received a registration certificate for
My body to be donated to Inje University of Medical
Science

Had a solo exhibition in the U.S.
The paintings has been kept for another solo exhibition
someday,
But now, to send them away, took photos with my nephew
Seon-moon

The mind that has been flowing, shaking distorted the paintings
Though shameful intentions discovered it can't help with the longing

Put the memories in the painting poem collection Flowing and Shaking Joy,

New owners will meet, the paintings of my another self
Now with blessings and joy, consoled my mind to free them
Finally a flowery gracious smile creeps in

Finally will I be able to shake off regrets and flow them away

Author Hyang Yeong Lee Lisa Lee
Haeundae, May 2024

차례

02 _ 프리다 칼로와 그녀 Frida Kahlo and She

차례

03 _ 그 분의 뜻을 따라서 Following His Will

호르고 흔들리는 기쁨 Flowing and Shaking Joy

04 _ 꽃 속에 잠들고 Daughter Fallen Asleep In the Flowers

차례

05 _ 너를 향한 기도 The Prayer Of Orientation Toward You

이향영 Lisa Lee

흐르고 흔들리는 기쁨 Flowing and Shaking Joy

06 _ 물로 그린 꽃 Water Drawn Flower

차례

07 _ 마지막 사랑의 축제를 The Festival of the Last Love

1

만남을 위한 단잠
Sweet Sleeping for Meeting

꽃의 대립

Flowers' Confrontation

꽃의 대립

네가 일어나면, 나는 누울게
네가 누우면, 나는 일어나고 싶어져

모순된 자리가, 정점인 우리의 관계

Flowers' Confrontation

If you get up, I will lie down
If you lie down, I get wanted to get up

The ironic positions, the peak of our relationship

그대 향한 그리움

Longing Toward Thee

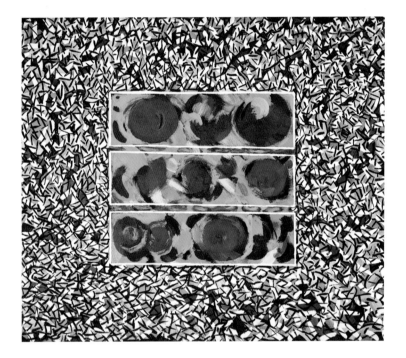

그대 향한 그리움

그대 향한,
붉은 상처가 깊이 뿌리내린
그 씨앗 하나, 가슴에서 꺼내

그대 지우면, 되살아나는 지독한 그리움

Longing Toward Thee

Toward thee,
Crimson injury rooted deeply down
That one seed, taking out from the heart

If erase thee, revives the tenacious longing

그림이 그린 시의 노래

A Painting Drawn Song of a Poem

그림이 그린 시의 노래

그리움은, 추상화를 그리고
보고픔은, 시를 쓰고
그대를 부르는, 노래는 바람이 되고

A Painting Drawn Song of a Poem

The longing, drew an abstract painting
The wishing to see, wrote a poem
Calling out thee, the song became a wind

끝없이 헌신적인 사랑

Endlessly Devoted Love

끝없이 헌신적인 사랑

당신의, 단잠을 위해
밤마다, 마을로 내려오는 수호천사

끝없이, 헌신적인 위대한 당신의 사랑

Endlessly Devoted Love

For your, sweet sleep
Every night, to the village descends the guardian angel

Endlessly, devoted great your love

내 안의 그대

Thou Within Me

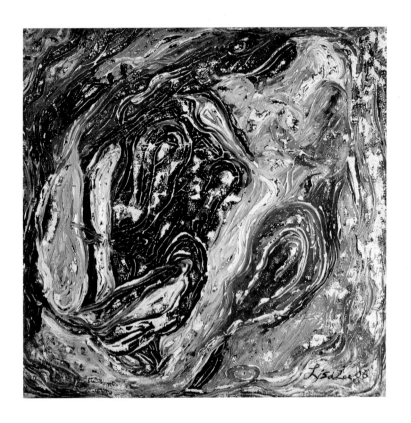

내 안의 그대

내 안의 그대는, 변화를
싫어하는 사랑, 그대는
내 몸에, 무늬로 프린트된 걸작품

Thou Within Me

Thou within me, the change
Hating love, Thou
In my body, printed in patterns a masterpiece

내부에서 피어나는 사랑

From Within Rising Love in Bloom

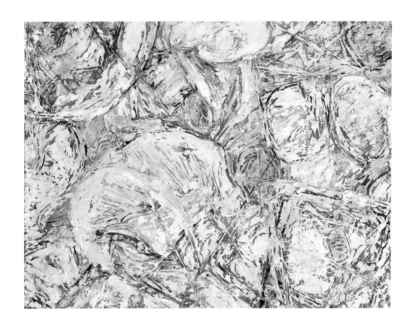

내부에서 피어나는 사랑

어떤 사물은, 오름행 계단을 만들고
오장육부로 키워낸, 향기 중 향기로

당신께 올려드리는, 기쁨은 중심의 사랑으로

From Within Rising Love in Bloom

Some objects, ascending steps make
By all the intestines reared to birth, the perfume among
the perfumes

To you dear raising as an offering, the gladness into
the center of love

너와 나의 고리
Rings for You and Me

너와 나의 고리

내 안에, 너의 세상이 있고
너 안에, 나의 세상이 있고

우리 사랑은, 고리로 연결되고

Rings for You and Me

Within me, is your world
Within you, is my world

Our love, gets tied in rings.

너와 나의 다른 세상

A Different World for You and Me

너와 나의 다른 세상

너는, 너의 세상에 흰 얼굴로
나는, 나의 세상에 살빛 얼굴로

언제나, 영혼으로 만나는 우리의 순간들

A Different World for You and Me

You, as a white face in your world
I, as a flesh color face in my world

Always, as a soul meeting moments for us

멈춘 지구 꽃사랑

Paused Earth Flower Love

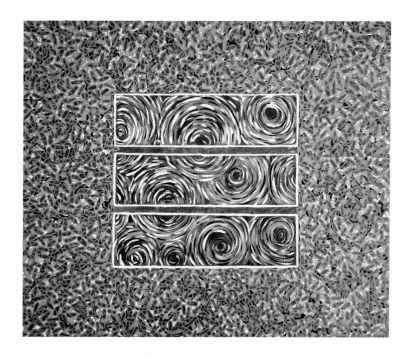

멈춘 지구 꽃사랑

하늘 닮은, 보랏빛 세포들
멈추어진 곳마다, 튼튼히 배양된

건강한 새 생명, 우주를 노래해

Paused Earth Flower Love

Resembling the sky, violet cells
Everywhere paused, stoutly cultured

Healthy new lives, sings the universe

그 사람이 그리워

Missing Thee

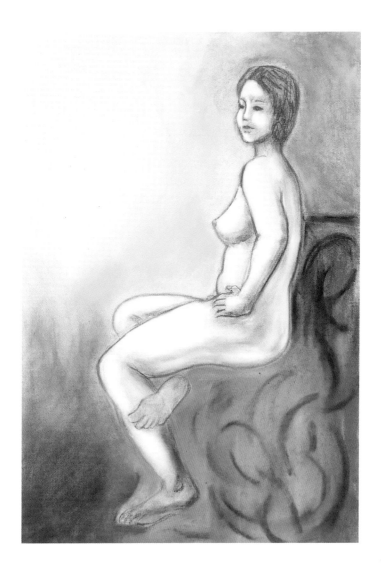

그 사람이 그리워

그이가 그리워서
마음을 지웠는데

어느새, 내 마음속에 자리한 그이!

Missing Thee

For missing thee
My mind erased though
In no time, inside my mind occupied thou

두 사람이 한 몸이 된 꽃

Two People Became One Body of Flower

두 사람이 한 몸이 된 꽃

커플이, 한 곳을 바라보는 자리
천연향, 꽃나무 한 그루
부부는, 한 몸이 되어가는 사랑 나무!

Two People Became One Body of Flower

A couple, looking on at one place
Natural perfume, flower of one tree
Husband and wife, one body becoming a love tree!

사랑의 과녁을

The Mark of Love

사랑의 과녁을

사랑은, 노력으로 만나고
사랑은, 희생으로 만나고
사랑은, 끝이 없는 진행형!

The Mark of Love

The love, met by effort
The love, met by sacrifice
The love, an endless progressive tense!

펜스 너머는 위험해

Dangerous Beyond the Fence

펜스 너머는 위험해

그리움은 왜 멀리 있을까?
펜스 너머, 저 바다 너머로

위험해도 따라가는, 그리움 하나!

Dangerous Beyond the Fence

Why will my longing be far?
Beyond the fence, toward beyond that sea

Dangerous as it is still following, the longing is one

만남을 위한 단잠

Sweet Sleeping for Meeting

만남을 위한 단잠

사랑하는 그대여,
꿈속에서라도 만나고파,

밤마다 천사가 되어 찾아가네,

Sweet Sleeping for Meeting

Thee that I love,
Even in the dream wishing to see,

Every night become I an angel to see thee

마음은 새처럼 자유로

The Mind Like a Bird to the Freedom

마음은 새처럼 자유로

그대는, 새가 되어 날아가도
너는, 그대를 기다리는 새가 되어

영혼은, 새처럼 자유롭게 기쁨이 차오르네

The Mind Like a Bird to the Freedom

Thou, become a bird and fly away though
You, become a bird waiting for thee

The soul, like a bird freely does the gladness rise up

모습은 그대를 위해서

My Appearance for Thee

모습은 그대를 위해서

새가 되어 날아간 그대,
그대 그리워,
새를 곁에 두었고,

의인화된 새처럼, 그대와 네가 함께하네!

My Appearance for Thee

Thou became a bird and flew away,
Longing for thee,
Left birds nearby,

Like personified birds, thou and you are together!

내면의 아름다움

Inner Aspect Beauty

내면의 아름다움

생각 속에도, 꽃은 피어나고
외면의 꽃은, 내면의 아름다움으로

사랑을 꽃처럼 가꾸어, 선물하고픈 마음

Inner Aspect Beauty

Even in thinking, the flower blooms out and
The outer aspect flower, by its inner aspect beauty

The love like a flower cultivates, in the mind wishing a
gift to give

무지개 사랑

Rainbow Love

무지개 사랑

끝이 없는, 엄마의 사랑!
평화를 꿈꾸는, 딸의 사랑!
모녀의 사랑은, 완전한 사랑!

머리카락이, 무지개의 꿈이 된 사랑!

Rainbow Love

Endless, mother's love!
Peace dreaming, daughter's love!
Mother and daughter's love, perfect love!

The hairs, the love that became the rainbow's dream!

흐르고 흔들리는 기쁨

Flowing and Shaking Joy

● Lisa Lee

2

프리다 칼로와 그녀

Frida Kahlo and She

마음속에 새긴 그림

A Drawing Carved Inside the Mind

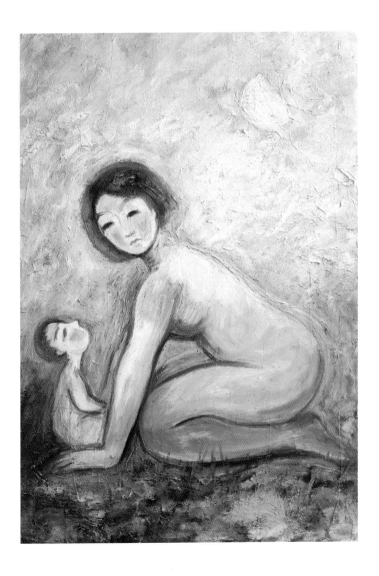

마음속에 새긴 그림

아가야, 엄마하고 놀자
엄마는, 우리 아가와 놀 때가
최고로, 기쁘고 즐겁고 행복해

아가는 엄마의 마스터피스!
엄마는 우리 아가의 소우주!

A Drawing Carved Inside the Mind

Baby, play with your mother
Your mother, at the time with our baby playing
The highest, excited and joyous and happy

A baby a mother's masterpiece
A mother a baby's little universe.

먼 거리감

Far Distant Feeling

먼 거리감

그대는, 나의 둘도 없는 친구
언제나, 하나인 둘로
둘이 된, 하나인 것을

너무나 먼 거리감의, 가까운 그대

Far Distant Feeling

Thou, a friend none another
Whenever, as two in one
Be two, into one

Too far distant feeling, thou near

면역세포

NK Cell

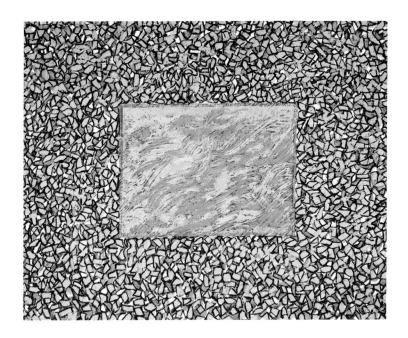

면역세포

NK Cell
노랑 옷 입은, 면역세포들
옥색 배양 공간에서, 자라난 세포들

새 생명, 선물로 지은 새 옷 입고 웃네

Immunocyte

NK Cell
Yellow clothes wearing, immuno-cells
In Jade green cultivation space, raised cells

New lives, in new clothes made as gift laugh

바다의 날개 윤슬

The Sea's Moonlit Wing Wavelets

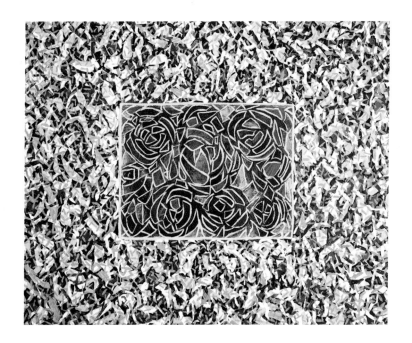

바다의 날개 윤슬

바다의, 몸에는
은가루, 찬란한 날개가 있고
윤슬은, 달 가루 장미로 창조되기도

The Sea's Moonlit Wing Wavelets

The sea's, body
Silver powdered, dazzling wings has
The moonlit wavelets, by the moon powdered roses
created too

엄마와 아들
Mother and Son

엄마와 아들

원래는, 하나였다가
잠시, 둘로 갈라졌다가
본향에서, 다시 만난 어느 모자

Mother and Son

Originally, was one and then

For a short while, was separated into two

In the original home town, met again a mother and her

son

자유

Freedom

자유

몸이 뜨거워지면, 나체가 될 것
빈 손길로, 차가운 가슴을 열고
꽃잎 입술로, 사랑을 창조할 것

그는 사랑이었고, 그는 부활이었고

Freedom

If the body gets hot, naked will it be
By empty hand gesture, will the cold heart open and
By flower leaf lips, the love creating will be

He was the love and, he was the revival and

초록 눈의 아들을 품고

Embracing Green Eyed Son

초록 눈의 아들을 품고

앙리 마티스의 그림을, 닮은 초록 눈
사랑의 빛은, 위대해서 볼 수 없고
창조하는 권능은, 걸작품을 만드는 것

엄마의 사랑은, 신의 사랑을 닮은 마스터피스

Embracing Green Eyed Son

Henri Matisse's painting, resembling green eyes
The love's light, too great to look at and
The power of creating talent, making a masterpiece

Mother's love, God's love resembling masterpiece

꽃을 품은 소녀

A Flower Hugging Girl

꽃을 품은 소녀

소녀는 꽃보다 예쁘고
소녀는 꽃보다 사랑스럽고

소녀가 꽃이고, 꽃은 소녀였네!

A Flower Hugging Girl

The girl prettier than a flower
The girl lovelier than a flower

The girl is a flower, the flower was the girl!

꿈속의 사닥다리

The Ladder Inside the Dream

꿈속의 사닥다리

땅에서 하늘로 연결된
야곱의 사닥다리처럼
꿈에서도 좋을
네가 간 그 길, 그리움이 된 그 길

나도 가고 있고, 내 소망도 따라가네

The Ladder Inside the Dream

From the land toward the sky connected
Jacob's ladder like
Even in the dream would good
Be the road you went along, a longing became that road

I too am going along, so is my wish following on

나의 또 다른 심장

Mine Another Different Heart

나의 또 다른 심장

어느 날, 엄마의 심장이 된 딸
붉은 심장에서, 초록으로 자란 딸

엄마의 계절이, 그리움을 품은 딸

Mine Another Different Heart

Some other day, a mother's heart the daughter became
From crimson heart, into green grew the daughter

The mother's season, the longing hugging daughter

엄마 머리 안 초록 소녀

The Green Girl Inside a Mother's Head

엄마 머리 안 초록 소녀

엄마에게 딸은, 분신이고!
엄마에게 딸은, 자신이고!
모녀는, 둘이서 하나가 되네!

The Green Girl Inside a Mother's Head

To mother the daughter, another self!
To mother the daughter, herself!
Mother and daughter, by the two become one!

음악이 있는 회색 풍경

Gray Scenery with Music

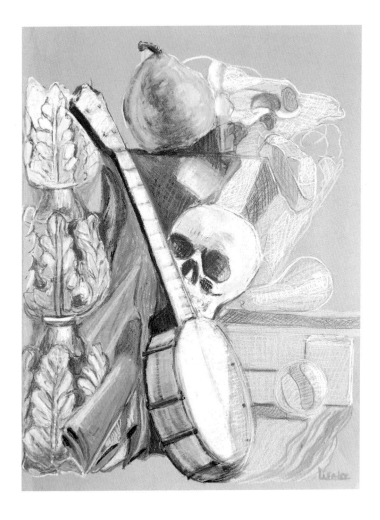

음악이 있는 회색 풍경

너는 과일을 들을 수 있니?
너는 음악을 먹을 수 있니?

아무튼 너는 볼 수 있어, 그리움을!

Gray Scenery with Music

Can you listen to the fruit?
Can you eat the music?

Anyway you can see, the longing!

정다운 꽃병

Affectionate Vase

정다운 꽃병

화병도, 두 개 있으면
다정한, 이웃이 되고
든든한, 친구가 되네!

Affectionate Vase

Even flower bottles, if two
Affectionate, neighbors become and
Reliable, friends become!

프리다 칼로와 그녀

Frida Kahlo and She

프리다 칼로와 그녀

프리다 칼로를, 사랑한 그녀
멕시코 프리다의, 옛집 정원에서
그녀는, 새들을 프리다처럼 만났네

Frida Kahlo and She

Frida Kahlo, loved she
Mexico Frida's, old house garden thence
She, the birds met like Frida

환상 속의 기쁘미

Ms Joy in Fantasy

환상 속의 기쁘미

기쁘미, 너는 고요이다
기쁘미, 너는 평화이다

평화가, 고요히 걸어오고 있다

Ms Joy in Fantasy

Ms Joy, you are quietness
Ms Joy, you are peace

The peace, is quietly coming on foot

PAUL EUBIN LEE

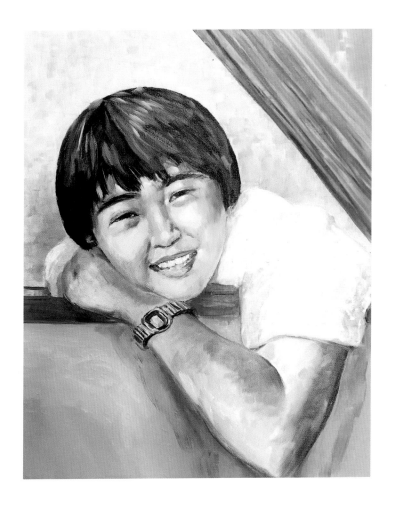

PAUL EUBIN LEE

물새처럼 산새처럼 외계로 간 너
너는 해가 갈수록, 고통의 그리움
나의 작업은, 그대의 존재가 되어

기억해 가는, 시와 그림과 소설이 되네

Paul Eubin Lee

Like a water bird like a mountain bird to an outer space
you went
　　You the more years pass by, the painful longing
　　My work, becomes thy existence

　　Going on remembering, poems and paintings and novels
become oh

엄마와 딸

Mother and Daughter

엄마와 딸

엄마의 품은
사랑과 평화
아가는 우주

엄마는 품 안의 우주와 사랑을 나누고

Mother and Daughter

Mother's hugging breast is
Love and peace
The baby is the universe

The mother shares love with the universe in her breast

만들어 가는 자유

Freedom Going on Making

만들어 가는 자유

춤을 추는, 시간에는
외로움이, 비켜 가고

그이의, 영혼과 하나가 되네

Freedom Going on Making

A dance dancing, time
Loneliness, goes aside and

With his, soul becomes one oh

흐르고 흔들리는 기쁨
Flowing and Shaking Joy ● Lisa Lee

3

그 분의 뜻을 따라서

Following His Will

줄기세포

Stem Cell

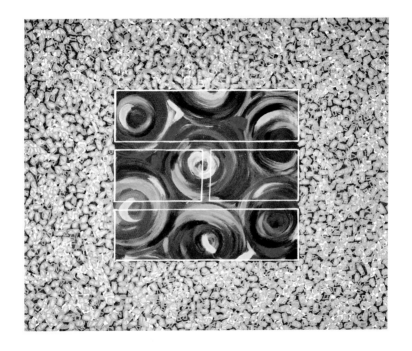

줄기세포

미움은 흘려보내고
배양으로 자란 세포들
스템 셀로 살아남아서

당신의 건강을 생성시키는 고마운 그대!

Stem Cell

Letting the hatred flow away
Cells that grew in cultivation
Remaining alive as stem cells

Grateful thou for generating your health!

그날이 오면은

If That Day Comes

그날이 오면은

계절은 우주를, 돌고 돌아
언젠가, 그날이 오면은

너는 그분을 만나리, 그곳에서

If That Day Comes

The season the universe, turning around and around
Some time, if that day comes

May you that man meet, at that place

다정한 갈등

Affectionate Conflict

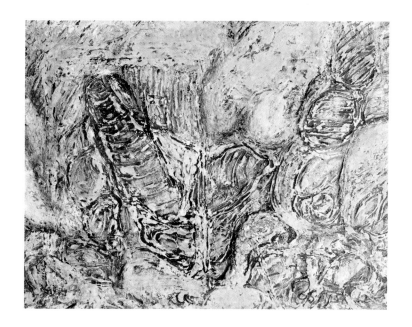

다정한 갈등

땅과 하늘을, 잇는 계단
너와 나를, 연결하는 관계

다정해서, 슬픈 우리의 갈등

Affectionate Conflict

The ground and the sky, linking steps
You and me, connecting relationship

Being affectionate, sad is our conflict

물결의 속삭임

Water Waves Whisper

물결의 속삭임

물결이, 흔들리다
꽃잎이 된, 시와 노래의 리듬

그대 기다리다, 상처가 된 꽃잎 가슴

Water Waves Whisper

Water waves, swaying and then
Flower leaves becoming, poem and song's rhythm,

For Thee waiting, injured got the flower leaf heart.

이별이 없는 이별

Parting Without Parting

이별이 없는 이별

이별이 없는 이별이란
서로의 영혼에 사랑이
영원으로 조각된 형상

Parting Without Parting

Parting without parting is
In each other's soul the love
Into eternity carved figure

다정한 내부의 갈등을

The Sweet Inner Conflict

다정한 내부의 갈등을

너는, 나를 떠나서 혼자가 되고
나는, 너를 떠나서 홀로가 되고
우리는, 한때 다정했었고

서로는, 이제 만날 수 없는 인연이 되고

The Sweet Inner Conflict

You, left me and became alone
I, left you and became by myself and
We, were sweet once and

Each other, at last unseeable became our ties and

마음속의 거울

A Mirror inside the Mind

마음속의 거울

내 속의, 나를 보면
실망의 44계단이고, 가끔은
거울 속의 네가, 멋져 보이기도

A Mirror inside the Mind

Within me, looking at me
The 44 steps of disappointment, at times
You inside the mirror, look even cooler

마음은 외롭고 몸은

The Mind Is Lonely and the Body

마음은 외롭고 몸은

외로울 때는, 바닷가에서
몸과 마음이, 자연이 되는 것

자연 안에서, 고개 숙여 겸손을 배우네

The Mind Is Lonely and the Body

When lonely, by the sea
The body and the mind, becoming nature

Within nature, bowing the head learn humbleness

멀리 있는 그리움

Longing at Distance

멀리 있는 그리움

곁에서, 더 보고 싶던 마음
멀어져, 그칠 줄 알았는데
단절은, 짙은 그리움이 되었고

언젠가, 나도 천국 시민이 되겠네!

Longing at Distance

By being near, the mind wanting to see more
By being distant, presumably would stop though
The severance, became a deep longing

Someday, I too will become a citizen of heaven!

무거우나 가벼운 생각

Heavy but Light Thinking

무거우나 가벼운 생각

내가, 못나서 떠났다면 이해가 되고
나를, 감당 못해 떠났다면 용서가 안 되고

기다리는 마음은 포기를 모르고, 우짤끼고?

Heavy but Light Thinking

I, because poor-looking if partied understandable
Me, because uncontrollable if partied unforgivable

Waiting mind never knows about giving up, so what will
you do?

상처가 힘이 되어
The Scar Became Power

상처가 힘이 되어

어두운, 너 몸의 상처가
힘이 되어, 밝은 에너지로

꿈이 자라고 있는, 치유의 반응

The Scar Became Power

Dark, scar on your body
Became power, in a bright energy
The dream growing up, healing's response

땅의 변질

The Deterioration of the Ground

땅의 변질

아직 땅의 희망이 살아있어
변질이 된 흙에도, 연두색은 돋아나고
내일은 푸르름의 계절이 싱그러울

찬란한 땅의 역사를 당대는 기록하리라

The Deterioration of the Ground

The ground's hope still remains alive so
Even in the deteriorated dirt, the yellow green sprouts
Tomorrow the season of greenness to be fresh

And brilliant earth's history the contemporary age will
record

땅의 변형

The Deformation of the Ground

땅의 변형

흘러넘치는 오물로
괴로워하는 흙의 가족들
살아가는 것이 두려워진 오늘

땅은 변형의 몸으로 외치네
제발 좀 사랑하며 살게 해달라고

The Deformation of the Ground

By overflowing filth
Annoyed families of the dirt
Feared of being alive today

The ground shouts out with its deformed bodies
Please let me live in love

땅의 변화

The Changes of the Ground

땅의 변화

변하지 않는 것이 없고
공기와 바람이 변화하더니
땅도 병든 색채로 몸살을 앓고

지구가 흘리는 눈물로 가슴이 타네

The Changes of the Ground

There is nothing that does not change and
I saw the air and wind change
The ground also has body aches in sick colors

My heart aches by the tears this planet is shedding

얼굴 없는 얼굴의 혼

The Soul of the Faceless Face

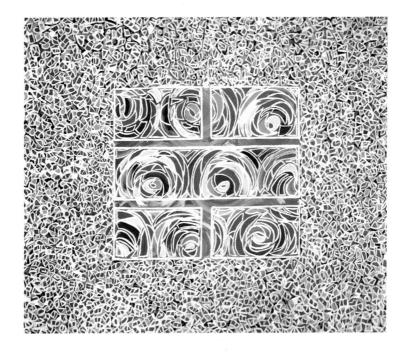

얼굴 없는 얼굴의 혼

내 마음 안에 네가 있다,
너를 보기 위해 가야겠다,
모험의 힘을 켜는 중이다,

장미의 가시가 그리움의 평화다,

The Soul of the Faceless Face

In my mind are you,
To see you will I have to go,
I am putting on the power of adventure,

The thorns of the roses are the peace of the longing,

대책 없이 쓸쓸함

Hopelessly Lonesome

대책 없이 쓸쓸함

찬란하고 화려한 계절은
왠지 쓸쓸하고, 눈물이 나서
내가 나를 모르는, 동굴로 숨고 싶어져

나를 찾는, 황금 발자국이 가까이 오네

Hopelessly Lonesome

Brilliant and magnificent season
Why lonely and, tears welling so
that I don't know myself, want to hide into a cave so

Looking for me, the golden foot marks coming nearer
oh

황금 동굴 속에서

Inside the Golden Cave

황금 동굴 속에서

그대가 그리워 찾아간 황금 동굴
영혼의 고향엔, 검은 얼굴도 있지만
용기와 인내로 찾아간 모험심

황금빛에 싸인, 그대는 황금 왕관
내 가슴이 벅차고 설레는, 황금 동굴의 나라

Inside the Golden Cave

The golden cave thou longed for and visited
In the hometown of the soul, are yet black faces as well
The adventurous mind visiting there with courage and
patience

Surrounded by golden lights, thou are a golden crown
My heart with excitement filling up, golden nation of
cave

비뚤어지다

Distorted

비뚤어지다

마음이 삐뚤어지더니
몸 자세 삐뚤어지더니
카메라가 흔들리더니

지구의 눈이 정신 못 차리고
세상이 온통 비뚤어져 버렸네

Distorted

The mind got distorted
The posture got distorted
The camera got shaky

The eye of this planet lost its senses
The world all over got distorted

그분의 뜻을 따라서

Following His Will

그분의 뜻을 따라서

당신에게 바치는, 형제의 기도
무릎 꿇고 온몸으로 올리는, 두 팔의 열정
로댕의 칼레의 시민을, 닮은 기도의 시민

저들의 호흡은, 당신 것이 된 기도의 꽃!

Following His Will

To dear you offering, prayers by the brothers
Kneeling and raising their entire bodies, two arms' pas-
sion
Rodin's Monument to the Burghers of Calais, resembling
citizens of prayers

Their breaths, became yours the flower of a prayer

흐르고 흔들리는 기쁨

Flowing and Shaking Joy

● Lisa Lee

4

꽃 속에 잠들고

Daughter Fallen Asleep
In the Flowers

꿈의 씨앗 꽃피우리

The Dream Seed Will Bloom a Flower

꿈의 씨앗 꽃피우리

작은 창안에서, 키운 꿈
그 씨앗은, 큰 나무가 되고
불후의 명작이 되는

그대의 위대한 기쁨이 되리라

The Dream Seed Will Bloom a Flower

Inside the little window, grew the dream
The seed, will a big tree become and
Will an immortal masterpiece become

Will surely thine great gladness become

노란 계절의 환희

The Mirth of Yellow Season

노란 계절의 환희

봄은 노란, 빛으로 숨어오는가?
봄은 초록, 빗물로 찾아오는가?

봄은 환희로, 춤추며 오는 계절인가?

The Mirth of Yellow Season

The spring yellow, coming in light hiding?
The spring green, coming to visit in raindrops?

The spring in mirth, coming season dancing?

막춤의 자유로운 행복

Uncontrolled Happiness of Free Dance

막춤의 자유로운 행복

넓디넓은 곳이나, 좁은 곳이나
어제도 오늘도, 신나는 춤을 추고

내일은 하늘가는, 기쁨의 춤을 추리라

Uncontrolled Happiness of Free Dance

Whether in the wide and wide place, or narrow place
Yesterday or today too, thrilling dances dance and

Tomorrow to sky going, dances of excitement will I dance

노랑머리, 초록머리

Yellow head, Green Head

노랑머리, 초록머리

색채 화가, 앙리 마티스의 그림이
연상되는, 목이 긴 두 소녀의 이미지

화려한 색깔은, 기쁨을 창조하는 계절 사랑

Yellow head, Green Head

Color painter, Henri Matisse's paintings
Reminded, two long necked girl images

Splendid colors, gladness creating season's love.

모녀는 꽃 속에 잠들고

Mother and Daughter Fallen Asleep In the Flowers

모녀는 꽃 속에 잠들고

꽃동산, 향기 이불 덮고
모녀는, 눈과 마음을 쉬고

달콤한 꽃물에 취해서, 꽃 꿈을 꾸네

Mother and Daughter Fallen Asleep In the Flowers

On a flowery hill, covered with a perfume quilt
The mother and the daughter, resting eyes and minds

Intoxicated with sweet flower water, dreaming of a
flower dream

특별한 모녀

Special Mother and Daughter

특별한 모녀

엄마의 가슴이 낳은 딸
동양과 서양이 만난 독특한 인연
딸의 하늘이 된 파란 눈의 엄마

영원히 함께할 특별한 우리 사랑!

Special Mother and Daughter

The daughter a mother's heart bore
The unique tie the East and the West met
The blue eyed mother who became the daughter's sky

Our special love that will always be together!

모르는 단장

Decoration Not Known

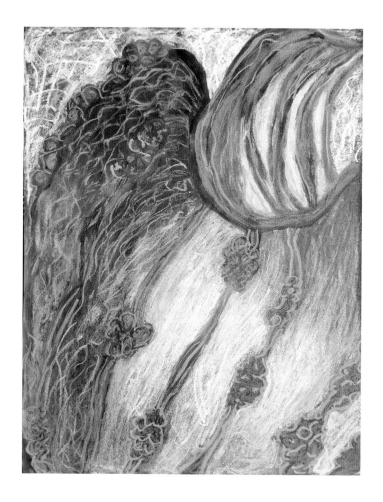

모르는 단장

자기의 내면을 깨끗이 단장하고,
자신의 외면도 예쁘게 단장하고,

자신 있게, 사랑하며 멋지게 사는 거야,

Decoration Not Known

Her inside aspect cleanly decorating,
Her outside aspect also prettily decorating,

With confidence, yes that's it Live loving cool,

모자의 어떤 환희

A Mirth of Mother and Son

모자의 어떤 환희

함께 있으면, 꽉 차오르는 기쁨!
떨어져 있어도, 채워지는 환희!
꽃과 나비처럼, 기쁨을 가꾸는 모자!

A Mirth of Mother and Son

If being together, the gladness fully rising up!
Even being separated, the mirth getting filled up
Like flowers and butterflies, mother and son cultivating
their gladness!

벗고도 당당한 그녀는

She Naked But Proud

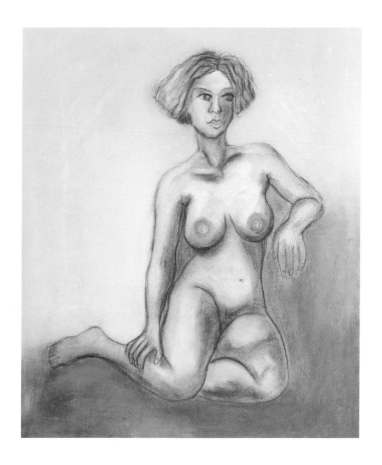

벗고도 당당한 그녀는

벗으면 더욱 당당해지는, 그녀!
원색과 탄력의 매력으로,
아름다운 곡선을 자랑하는,

흑인 모델, 그녀는 아바타 힐로!

She Naked But Proud

If taking off her clothes getting prouder, she!
By prime colors and the attraction of resilience,
Taking pride in her beautiful curvy lines,

The black model, she is Avatar Hillo!

저 밝은 곳을 향하여

Toward That Bright Place

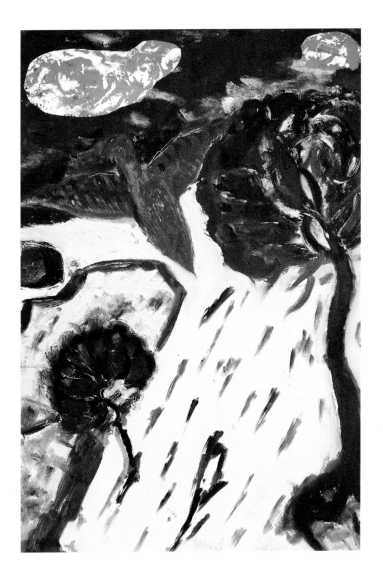

저 밝은 곳을 향하여

너는 떠도는, 구름을 꿈꾸고
나는 새처럼, 자유롭게 날고 싶고

검은 나무는, 푸른 계절을 그리워하네

Toward That Bright Place

You the floating, clouds dream and
Like a bird I, want to fly freely

The dark tree, longing for the green season

코스타리카 그 폭포와 숲

Costa Rica Forest of That Waterfall

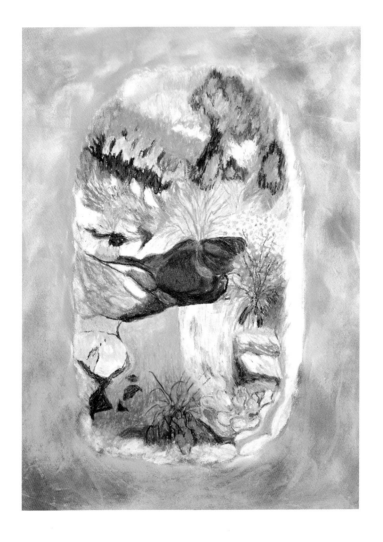

코스타리카 그 폭포와 숲

코스타리카, 그 숲속에서
블루색 왕나비, 네 머리 위에 앉았고
폭포는 장엄한, 음악을 켰었지

야외온천장은, 꿈의 천국이었을까?

Costa Rica Forest of That Waterfall

Costa Rica, in that forest
Blue color king butterfly, on my head sat and
The waterfall solemn, music had played

Outdoor hot springs resort, was the dream heaven?

휴식은 단꿈으로

Resting into a Sweet Dream

휴식은 단꿈으로

풍만할수록, 쉼이 그리운 건
그대 그리워, 단꿈을 꾸는 것

살이 불어날수록, 휴식은 달콤하기만 하네

Resting into a Sweet Dream

The plumper, the more resting missing
For thee missing, dreaming a sweet dream

The more blown up the flesh, the sweeter the resting

목적이 같은, 다정한 자매

With the Same Goal, Sweet Sisters

목적이 같은, 다정한 자매

라벤더와 아이리스를 닮은 향기
꿈과 소망을, 저 먼 곳에 두고
욕심(옷)을 벗고, 자유를 누리는 자매

With the Same Goal, Sweet Sisters

Lavender and iris resembling perfume
Dreams and wishes, in the far distance leaving
Desires(clothes) taking off, freedom enjoying sisters

마음의 집
The House of My Mind

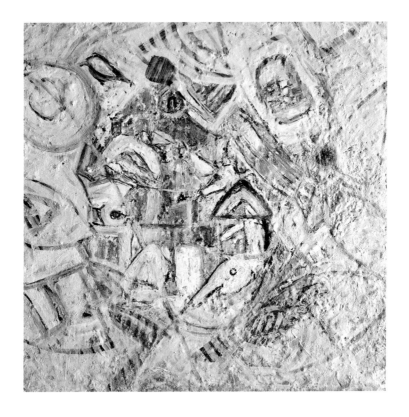

마음의 집

물고기들이 사는
내 마음의 집에는
낙엽과 자유가 함께

공존하는, 평화와 화해의 집이네

The House of My Mind

Fish living
In the house of my mind
Fallen leaves and freedom together

Co-existing, house of peace and reconciliation

난해한 계절

An Esoteric Season

난해한 계절

미세먼지가 덮어버린 그곳에
우리의, 아름다웠던 지난날이
빛을 잃고, 흩어진 추억의 조각들

난해한 계절 속에 보석이 되어 묻혀있네

An Esoteric Season

In the place the fine dust covered
Our, past days that had been beautiful
lost their lights, pieces of memories scattered

Buried inside the esoteric season as jewelry

난해한 그리움

An Esoteric Longing

난해한 그리움

빛이 스미어 탈색된 풍경처럼
만남이 가난해져 찾아온 이별
그대는 떠나고, 그리움만 남은

수상한 계절을 나는 견디고 있네

An Esoteric Longing

Like a scenery bleached by lights filtered out
The parting visited by impoverished meeting
Thou left, only longing remained

The suspicious season I am enduring

어떤 사랑

Some Love

어떤 사랑

눈을 감고 만나는 연인
영혼으로 만나는 즐거움은
변함이 없는, 깊고 높은 사랑

평화와 기쁨이, 잠잠한 영혼의 나라

Some Love

Lovers meeting with their eyes closed
Joy meeting by soul
Not changing, deep and high love

Peace and gladness, settled down nation of the soul

스피릿 댄스

Spirit Dance

흐르고 흔들리는 기쁨

스피릿 댄스

진달래가 핀 산의 꽃밭
분홍 춤을 추고파서
소풍 나온 영혼들

마냥 즐거운 스피릿 댄스!

Spirit Dance

Azalea bloomed mountain flower garden
Wanting to dance a pink dance
Picnic coming souls

The spirit dancers joyful to their hearts

흐르고 흔들리는 기쁨
Flowing and Shaking Joy

● Lisa Lee

5

너를 향한 기도
The Prayer Of Orientation
Toward You

검지가 피운 꽃

A Flower Bloomed by the Forefinger

검지가 피운 꽃

검지가 붓이 되어
장미로 피어난 아름다움
성 프란체스코의, 기도는
장미밭의 가시를 지웠다네

A Flower Bloomed by the Forefinger

The forefinger became a brush
and the beautifulness that bloomed into a rose
St. Francesco's, Prayer
Oh erased the thorns of rose garden

기도하는 소녀

A Praying Girl

기도하는 소녀

당신이, 폭소로 웃는
당신이, 박수로 웃은
당신이, 몸으로 웃는

당신의, 웃음꽃이 되고파요, 저는

A Praying Girl

You, laughing in a guffaw
You, laughing in an applause
You, laughing with your body

Your, flower of a laughter wish to be, I

기도하는 소년

A Praying Boy

기도하는 소년

그대가, 정말로 기뻤으면
그대가, 정말로 행복했으면
그대가, 정말로 즐거웠으면

그대를, 위해서 기도가 되고파요, 저는

A Praying Boy

Thou, if truly were glad,
Thou, if truly were happy
Thou, if truly had a good time

Thee, for a prayer wish to be, I

너를 향한 지향의 기도

The Prayer Of Orientation Toward You

너를 향한 지향의 기도

천 개의 촛불을 켜고
마음의 지향을
먼 곳의, 그대에게 두고

그대를 위해, 기도 하는 내 사랑아

The Prayer Of Orientation Toward You

Lighting a thousand candles
The orientation of the mind
In a distant place, to thine leaving

For thee, oh my praying love

누드로 드리는 기도

In Nude Offering a Prayer

누드로 드리는 기도

네, 모습 그대로
죄를 회개하고, 온 맘으로

무릎 꿇고, 맨몸으로 올려 드리는 기도

In Nude Offering a Prayer

You, just as you are
The sins repenting of, cordially
Knees kneeling, in a bare body raising and offering a
prayer

믿음은 바라는 것의 실상

Believing the Reality of Desiring Things

믿음은 바라는 것의 실상

믿음은, 바라는 것들의 실상인 것을
소녀는, 어제도 오늘도 내일도
믿음의 실상을 믿고, 기도로 기뻐하네

Believing the Reality of Desiring Things

Believing, desiring things' realities
The girl, yesterday also today also and tomorrow also
The believing's reality believing, in the prayer excited

부활

The Resurrection

부활

죽음은, 그분의 선물
죽음이, 기다리는 삶은
너무나도, 아름다운 것

부활이, 그분의 약속이기에

The Resurrection

Dying, his gift
Dying, waiting life
All too, beautiful thing

The Resurrection, owing to his promise

오직 그 길의 표징

Signs of Only That Way

오직 그 길의 표징

오직, 그 길만이 생명인데
흩어진, 회색 마음을
촛불이 켜진, 어두운 공간을

십자가 바늘로, 완성을 꿰매고 있는

Signs of Only That Way

Only, that way's a life though
Scattered, ash colored mind
The candle light lit, dark space

With the cross needles, sewing on its completeness

혼돈 속의 고요
The Stillness Within Chaos

혼돈 속의 고요

세상은 혼란스러워도
물고기 배속은, 요나*가 잠깐 살았던
안식처, 평화와 고요의 요람이었네

* 요나 : 성경에 나온 예언자. 주님을 피해 도망하던 중, 물고기 뱃 속에서 삼일 삼야
를 무사히 지냄

The Stillness Within Chaos

Though the world is chaotic
The fish's belly within, Jona* briefly lived
Haven, was the peace and stillness's cradle

* Jonah : A Biblical prophet, while escaping from the Lord, spent three days and
three nights safely within the belly of a fish.

당신이 선물한 사랑의 흔적

The Love Traces You Presented

당신이 선물한 사랑의 흔적

내가 힘들 때, 나를 업고 걸어주신
당신의 발자국마다, 내 검은 상처가

당신의 희생으로, 치유된 흔적이 눈부시네!

The Love Traces You Presented

When I was in difficulty, bearing me on your back and
walked
Everyone of your foot step, my black scar

By your sacrifice, the traces healed so dazzling!

머리가 땅에 닿는 기도

A Prayer with the Ground Reaching Head

머리가 땅에 닿는 기도

온몸과 맘으로 드리는, 자연 제단
땅도 하늘도 감화하는

정성이 유일신에게 올려지는 밀어!

A Prayer with the Ground Reaching Head

By all body and heart offering, natural altar
Even earth and heaven also influenced

The sincerity to the one and only God uplifted whisper

무지개 손과 초록 머리기도

The Prayer of Rainbow Hands and Green Head

무지개 손과 초록 머리기도

기도하는, 손과 가슴과 머리가
무지개의 상징으로, 해바라기를 돌리듯

빛의 힘으로, 물레방아로 돌아가는 너의 기도

The Prayer of Rainbow Hands and Green Head

Praying, hands and hearts and head
In a rainbow symbol, like turning a sunflower

In the power of light, your prayer turning in a water
mill

무지개의 기도

A Rainbow's Prayer

무지개의 기도

엄마가 있기에, 아들이 있고
아들이 있기에, 엄마가 있고

기도가 무지개 되어, 끝없는 약속의 사랑

A Rainbow's Prayer

Because there's mother, there's son
Because there's son, there's mother

The prayer becomes a rainbow, love of endless promise

빛의 꽃

The Light Flower

빛의 꽃

우주가, 그려낸 꽃
태양이, 그린 꽃
빛의 손으로, 그려진 꽃

성령이 피워낸, 치유의 꽃

The Light Flower

The universe, drawing out flower
The sun, drawn flower
By the hands of light, drawn flower

The holy spirit blooming out, healing flower

영혼의 안식을 위하여

For the Rest of Soul

영혼의 안식을 위하여

생각을, 높이 달아 놓고
마음은 늘, 그곳에 밝게 켜두고
오늘도 성실히, 그 길을 가고 있는

너는 십자가 그늘에서, 다시 태어났네

For the Rest of Soul

The thinking, hanging high up
The mind always, there put on bright
Today as well sincerely, going on the way

You in the shade of the cross, found born again

흐르고 흔들리는 기쁨 ● Liisa Lee

Flowing and Shaking Joy

6

물로 그린 꽃
Water Drawn Flower

물들어 가는 초록 계절

Getting Colored Green Season

물들어 가는 초록 계절

초록의 봄은, 우주에서 내려오고
혼돈의 봄 물결, 땅속에서 빠르고
빠른 걸음은, 그대가 내게로 오는

초록의 계절은, 그대와 내가 만나는 길

Getting Colored Green Season

The green's spring, from the universe descends and
The chaos's spring waves, Under the ground quick and
Quick footsteps, thou to me coming

The green's season, the road thou and I meet

물로 그린 꽃

Water Drawn Flower

물로 그린 꽃

물이, 그려낸 오묘한 꽃잎
그대 이름은 꽃별이, 우주에 핀
단 한 송이, 물로 그린 꽃잎

그대와 나 사이에서, 태어난 꽃

Water Drawn Flower

The water, drawn out mysterious flowers
Thine name the flower stars, in the universe bloomed
The only one bunch, water drawn flower leaf

Between thee and me, born the flower

물이 꽃이 된 그림

The Painting Water Became Flower

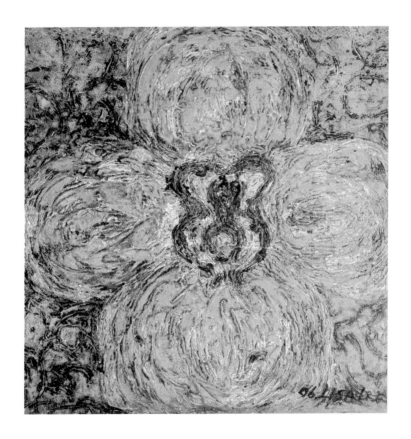

물이 꽃이 된 그림

옥색, 물꽃 곱게 피워
당신께, 드리고픈 꽃사랑
오매불망, 당신만 바라보는 꽃

그날까지 변치 않고, 기다림이 된 물꽃

The Painting Water Became Flower

Jade Green, water flower bloomed pretty so
To you dear, wishing to offer the flower love
Not forgetting day and night, flower looking at only you
dear

Until that day without changing, water flower that became a waiting

봄, 숨어서 오네

The Spring, Coming Hiding

봄, 숨어서 오네

봄은 숨어서 오는가?
미색이 핑크가 되고
아다지오로, 오다가 알레그로로 오고

그대 만날 때처럼 뛰어서, 숨이 차오르네

The Spring, Coming Hiding

Pale yellow makes pink and
In Adagio, coming to come in allegro

Running like when meeting thine, the breath filling up

봄을 품은 풍경

The Spring Embracing Scenery

봄을 품은 풍경

봄은, 찬란한 풍경을
꼭꼭, 숨겨놓고 있네
고운, 신부를 숨기듯

신부가, 옷 벗을 때 산천은 미소로

The Spring Embracing Scenery

The spring, the dazzling scenery
Solid hard, left being hidden
Graceful, bride hiding like

When the bride, her clothes taking off mountains and
rivers smile

봄이 흐르는 들판

The Spring Flowing Field

봄이 흐르는 들판

고운 봄이, 가득 담긴 들판은
야무진, 꿈의 절정이 흐르고

승리의 깃발은, 봄을 축하하네

The Spring Flowing Field

The gracious spring, filled up field
Ambitious, dream's acme flowing

The victory flag, congratulates on the spring

못난이 자화상

A Fool's Self-Portrait

못난이 자화상

나는 참 못생겼다.
나는 정말 못생겼다.

그래도, 너는 늘 미인이다.

A Fool's Self-Portrait

I am truly poorly shaped
I am really poorly shaped

However, you are always a beautiful person.

데스칸소 공원의 웃음

Laughter of Descanso Gardens

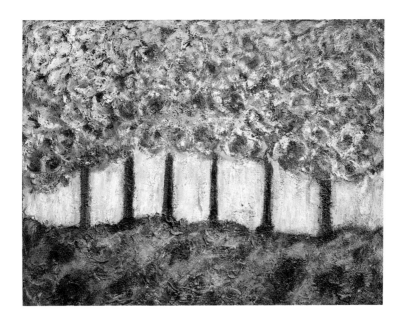

데스칸소 공원의 웃음

하늘 향해, 호호 하하 웃고 있는
울타리 장미의 박장대소
공원의 나들이 나온 사람들은

입술 꽃, 미소 꽃 만드는 향기가 되네

Laughter of Descanso Gardens

Toward the Sky, laughing ho ho ha ha
The fence roses' loud laughter in applause
People picnicking in the gardens

Become lip flowers, smile flowers making perfume

모든 색상과 자연은 아름다워

All Colors and Nature Are Beautiful

모든 색상과 자연은 아름다워

봄이 오는, 고운 색깔을 귀가 듣고
봄이 오는, 아픈 소리를 눈이 보고

봄은, 춤과 노래로 가슴 설레는 계절이네

All Colors and Nature Are Beautiful

The spring coming, pretty color shades the ears hear
The spring coming, painful sounds the eyes watch

The spring, for dances and songs a heart throbbing
season

몸속의 계절이 웃을 때

When The Season Within the Body Laughs

몸속의 계절이 웃을 때

몸속의, 장기들이 박장대소하고
뜨거워진, 마음이 표출되어

몸 밖으로, 나온 웃음이 춤추는 자유

When The Season Within the Body Laughs

Within the body, the organs laughing noisy clapping
Heated, heart displayed

Out from the body, coming the laughter dancing free—
dom

색상이 그려낸 계절 꿈

The Season Dream The Colors Painted

색상이 그려낸 계절 꿈

계절은, 색상으로 연주되고
그대는, 나를 조각하고, 작사는
오묘한, 작곡을 노래로 연출하네

The Season Dream the Colors Drew

The season, is played into colors
Thou, carve me and, the lyrics
Profound, music composition performs into a song

생명의 씨앗
The Seed of Life

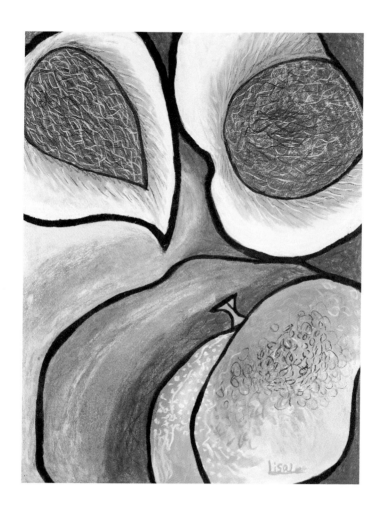

생명의 씨앗

창조되는 씨앗!
자라가는 생명!
신비로운 결실!

The Seed of Life

Being created seeds!
On growing life!
Mysterious fruition!

언덕의 꽃밭에서

In the Flower Field of the Hill

언덕의 꽃밭에서

꽃밭에 있으면, 향기에 취해서!
그대가 꽃이 된 듯, 착각에 빠지고!
모습은 영상처럼, 더 또렷해지는 그대!

In the Flower Field of the Hill

If in the flower field, drunken by the perfume!
Thou looking like a flower, into an illusion falling!
The appearance like a video, getting clearer thou!

홀로도 부끄러운 어머니

Even Alone Embarrassed Mother

홀로도 부끄러운 어머니

흰 등을, 보이고 앉아도
나체가, 부끄러운 어머니
그대가, 볼까 봐 얼굴을 가리네

Even Alone Embarrassed Mother

Her white back, exposed and sat yet
Her naked body, embarrassed mother
Fearing thou, may look at her covering her face

봄, 아파하며 오네

Spring, Coming in Pain

봄, 아파하며 오네

봄은 아파하면서 오는가?
천둥이 몇 차례 지나가고
폭풍이 흔들어 깨워서 오는가?

햇빛 이불 아래의 봄은 몸살을 앓네

Spring, Coming in Pain

Is spring coming in pain?
How many times did the thunder go by and
After the violent wind shook it to wake it up to come?

세상은 하나로

The World into One

세상은 하나로

어두움이, 너를 밝혀
뒤척이는, 등줄기
미색 달이 하얗게, 창에 걸려

그림자가 꽃으로 피었네

The World into One

The darkness, you brightens
Tossing and turning, backbone lines

The pale yellow moon in white, hanging on the window

흐르는 자연

Flowing Nature

흐르는 자연

구름은 노래하며 흐르고
하늘은 춤을 추며 흐르고
자연은 제 자리에서 시를 쓰고

그대 기다리는, 나도 한점 자연으로 흐르네

Flowing Nature

The clouds are flowing singing a song
The sky is flowing dancing a dance
Nature is writing a poem in its own place

Thine waiting, I too am flowing into a piece of nature

흐르고 흔들리는 기쁨
Flowing and Shaking Joy ● Lisa Lee

7

마지막 사랑의 축제를

The Festival of the Last Love

CSUN TIM

CSUN TIM

캘리포니아 주립대학교 노스릿지,
대학원의 Timothy 교수
그이가 좋아했던, 이 추상화만 보면

그 계절의 그리움이 요동치는 밀어!

CSUN TIM

California State University at Northridge
Prof. Timothy of graduate school
He liked this abstract painting, whenever I look at it

Heart-rending secret stories of that season's longing!

고해 속의 순결

The Purity Inside the Penance

고해 속의 순결

바다는, 온갖 오물을 품고
흑해에서, 억겁으로 숙성된
고해가, 피워낸 살뜰한 순결

The Purity Inside the Penance

The sea, bearing all kinds of filth
From the Black Sea, matured infinitely for a long time
The penance, eagerly put forth the purity

마음이 달려가는 길

A Road the Mind Goes Running

마음이 달려가는 길

김병기 화백이, 좋아했던 그림
그는, 천국으로 여행을 떠났고

그가 좋아했던 그림이, 말을 걸어오네

A Road the Mind Goes Running

The painter Kim Byung Gi, liked the drawing
He, left for traveling to heaven

The drawing he liked, came speaking to me

너는 나의 세상

You My World

너는 나의 세상

엄마는, 우주를 만들고
엄마는, 시간을 만들어
너와, 함께 하고 싶은데

어디로 가려고 애원하니?

You My World

A mother, makes the universe
A mother, makes time
With you, wishing to be together though

To where do you entreat to go?

그녀와 프리다 칼로

She and Frida Kahlo

그녀와 프리다 칼로

그녀는, 프리다 칼로를 그리고
프리다에게, 노래와 시를 선물하고파
칼로의 사랑, 디에고에 대한 시를 쓰네

She and Frida Kahlo

She, Frida Kahlo drew and
To Frida, wishing to present a song and poem
Kahlo's love, Diego a poem she writes about

그대 안의 나

I Within Thee

그대 안의 나

고운 명주로, 피륙을 짜서
그림을 무늬로 수놓아
아름다운 비단옷 입은

그대 안의 나로 살겠네

I Within Thee

With fine silk yarn, weave the drapery and
Embroider the painting as its patterns and
Wearing the beautiful silk clothes

Within thee will I live

둥글고 싶어지는 생각
Idea Wanting to be Rounded

둥글고 싶어지는 생각

모가 나고, 버려진 것이
둥글어져, 쓰임을 받고픈

갈망하는 둥근 꿈이여, 바람이여!

Idea Wanting to be Rounded

Angled, abandoned things
Getting rounded, wishing to be used

There aspiring round dream, there the wind!

마지막 사랑의 축제를

The Festival of the Last Love

마지막 사랑의 축제를

마지막이란, 슬픔일까?
마지막이란, 기쁨일까?
마지막이란, 이별 후 또 다른

설레는 구름 길이, 축제처럼 열려가는

The Festival of the Last Love

What is being the last, will it be a sadness?
What is being the last, will it be a gladness?
What is being the last, after parting again another

Like a mind throbbing way of the cloud, like festival
getting opened

이해할 수 없는 그리움

Not Understandable Longing

이해할 수 없는 그리움

어두움은, 빛을 꿈꾸고!
혼돈은, 사랑을 배양하고!

너는, 그대의 계절을 살아가고!

Not Understandable Longing

The darkness, dreams of light!
The chaos, cultivates love!

You, are living thy seasons!

일어나야지

Got to Get Up

일어나야지

언제까지 눈 감고 있을 거야?
눈을 떠봐, 일어나야지
나를 봐, 나를 좀 보란 말이야!

사랑이 식어가고 있잖아, 어떻해?

Got to Get Up

Until when will you stay with your eyes closed?
Open your eyes, got to get up
Look at me, I mean look at me!

The love is getting colder isn't it, what can I do?

하얀 묵상

White Meditation

하얀 묵상

네가, 이 지구별에 온 것은
당신을 위한, 향기가 되고
한 송이, 흰 묵상이 되어

당신을 기다리는, 신부가 되려고!

White Meditation

You, that came from the star of this planet
For you sweetheart, a perfume to become and
One bundle, white meditation to become and

For you waiting, bride to become!

곰 같은 너

You Like a Bear

곰 같은 너

너는 느려서 곰 같고
나는 빨라서 쥐 같고
세상이 아무리 혼란스러워도

우린 곰처럼 느리게 살아갔으면

You Like a Bear

You are slow so like a bear

I am quick so like a rat

No matter how chaotic the world is

We like a bear wish we could live slowly

모난 돌이 둥그러지면

If Angular Stones Gotten Circular

모난 돌이 둥그러지면

모난 사물들, 다듬어져
의미 있는, 기호로 태어나고

심장은 역사를 쓰고, 또 써가네

If Angular Stones Gotten Circular

Angular objects, shaped
Into meaningful, symbols born and

The hearts the history writing, writing again

미완성의 계절 스토리

A Season Story of Incompleteness

미완성의 계절 스토리

모든 것은 미완성,
사랑, 꿈, 인생, 오늘도
완성을 위해 일 하는, 그대의 당신

A Season Story of Incompleteness

All things incomplete,
Love, dream, living matter, today as well
For the completeness working, thine you

세월, 그날이 오면은

The Ages, If That Day Comes

세월, 그날이 오면은

몰래 숨겨둔 마음, 들썩이는
세월 안, 맨몸 안으로 네가 깊이
옮겨져, 환한 불로 세상을 밝히고

살아야 한다네, 살아가야 한다네

The Ages, If That Day Comes

In secret hidden mind, unsettled
Within the ages, and inward the bare body, deeply you
Gotten moved, in bright fire lighting up the world

Must live, must go on living

혼돈 속의 침묵

The Silence Within Chaos

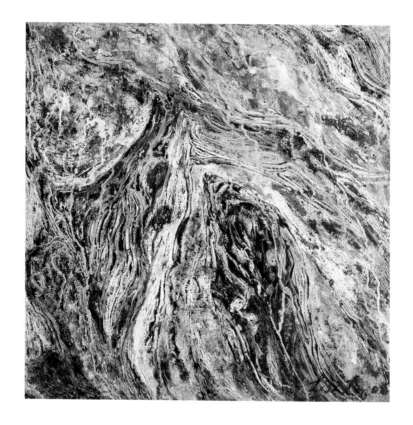

혼돈 속의 침묵

마르셀 뒤샹이 '변기'를 '샘'이라 했듯,
이 그림을 감상하는 분은, 이 그림의
제목을, 자유롭게 작명해 보시면 어떨까요?

The Silence Within Chaos

Just as Marcel Duchamp called the toilet a well,
Those who appreciate this painting, this painting's
Title, how about freely creating its name?

경계 너머의 하늘

The Sky Beyond the Boundary

경계 너머의 하늘

경계 너머의, 그곳에는
그대가 별이 되어 사는, 외계

나의 미래를, 그곳에 세웠네

The Sky Beyond the Boundary

The boundary beyond, there
Thou as a star living, outer space

My future, there erected

그림 공부와 자유

Painting Study and Freedom

그림 공부와 자유

공부는 왜 해야 하나?
그림은 왜 그려야 하나?
자유롭기 위해서일까?

아, 나비의 자유가 그립네!

Painting Study and Freedom

Why must study?
Why must paint?
For being free?

Ah, butterfly's freedom so missed

붙이고 싶은 마음

畵詩集을 준비하면서 그림을 볼 때마다 고마운 분들이 떠오른다.
LA에서 미술학원을 하셨던 강태호, 이영수 화백과 그리고
LACC에서 가르쳐 주셨던 올가, 헬렌, 스왓 교수
AIU – LA에서 지도해 주셨던 마이클, 스미스 교수
AIU-LONDON에서 아트폼 사진을 가르쳐주신 아가타 교수
CSUN에서 응원해 주신 티머시, 크리스티나 교수가
그림을 보면 오버랩되어 잊을 수 없는 추억을 소환해 준다.
열정적으로 가르쳐주셨는데, 더 잘못해 죄송하지만,
오늘 이 화집을 만들 수 있게 해주신 스승님들께 뜨거운 감사를
드린다.

미국에서 소망 소사이어티에 기증한 그림들과 전시회 때 팔린 그림들을 함께 책 속에 담을 수 없음이 너무 아쉽다.

당시에는 이렇게 畵詩集을 만들 줄 몰랐었기에 사진으로 남기지 못했다.

후회는 아무리 빨라도 늦다.

끝으로 짧은 기간에 번역을 맡아주신 이승희 교수와
복잡한 편집을 정리해서 책이 나오기까지 수고해주신
부산의 작가마을 출판팀에게 진심으로 감사드린다.

이향영 Lisa Lee

Words of Acknowledgement

While preparing this book of painting poems, every time I looked at my paintings, I thought of some honorable per—sons I was grateful for. Among those were artists Taeho Kang and Youngsoo Lee who ran an art institute in LA, Professors Olga, Helen, and Swat who taught me at LACC, and Professors Michael and Smith who mentored me at AIU—LA, and Professor Agatha who taught me Art forms of pictures at AIU—London. Above all, when I looked at my paintings, two unforgettable people came to mind as they overlapped the images; Professors Timothy and Christina who supported me at CSUN. These professors, who always taught me passionately, brought back many memories for me. I feel sorry for not being able to do better for them. Today, I would like to express my warm gratitude to all of these teachers, without whom I might not be able to create this book of painting poems.

Those paintings I donated to Somang Society and sold can-
not be included in this book, which is very unfortunate. At
that time, I had no idea that I would create a book like this
and leave behind those pictures. No matter how quickly I
regret it, I think it is too late.

Lastly, Professor Sunghee Lee took charge of the trans-
lation and completed it in a short period of time. And the
publishing team Writer's Village at Busan sorted out the
complicated editing, and took a lot of hard work to bring
this book to fruition. I am truly grateful to these people,
too.

Lisa Lee 이 향영